Margaret K. McElderry Books
An imprint of Simon & Schuster Children's Publishing Division
1230 Avenue of the Americas, New York, New York 10020
Text copyright © 2007 by Karma Wilson
Illustrations copyright © 2007 by Raúl Colón
Book design by Debra Sfetsios
The text for this book is set in Americana Std.
The illustrations for this book are rendered in ink and watercolor.
Manufactured in Mexico

ISBN-13: 978-0-689-86506-0

*To the troops who inspired this book—you are one of the most important
ingredients in our country. Thank you, and God bless.—K.W.*

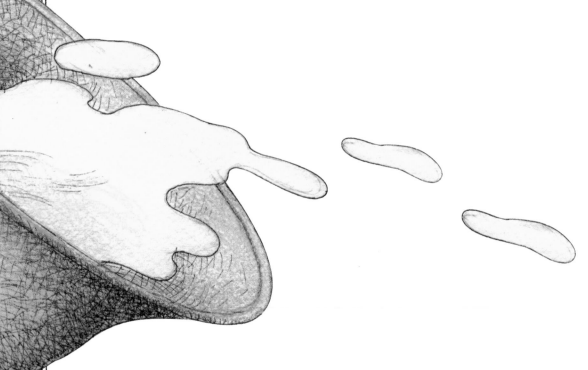

To the dedicated faculty and staff of Columbus Elementary School, Mt. Vernon, NY—R.C.

How to Bake an American Pie

by Karma Wilson

illustrated by Raúl Colón

margaret k. mcelderry books   new york london toronto sydney

Here's how to bake
an American pie

(first ever made on the

Fourth of July):

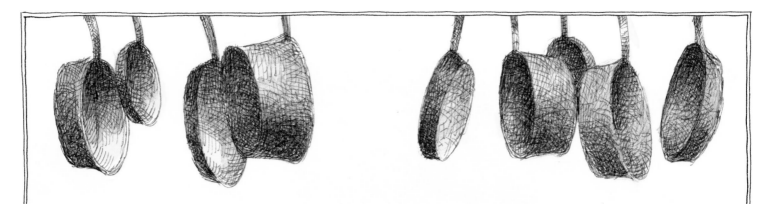

Preheat
the world until
fiery hot
with a
hunger
and **thirst**
to be
free.

Now find
a giant melting pot
on the shores
of a great
shining sea.

Pat out
a crust of
fruited plains,
then spread it
as far as you dare.
Fold in some fields
of amber grains,
enough for
all people
to share.

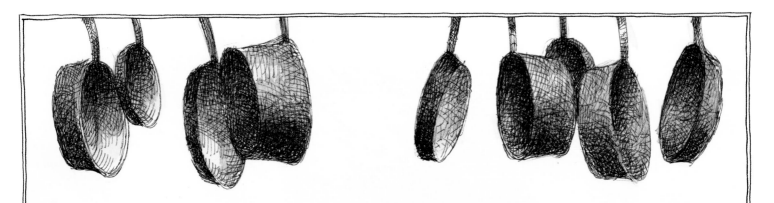

And though

it's getting

mighty high,

that's just

the **start** of

American pie!

Add
purple mountain majesties.
Measure
out meekness
and might.
Pour cupfuls
of courage,
as much as you please;
then leaven
with dawn's early light.

Ladle
out liberty fought for
and won
and justice for
both great and small.

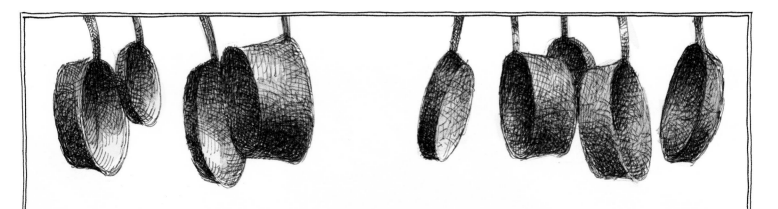

Whisk in
waterfalls
kissed by the sun;
then fold in
sweet
freedom
for all.

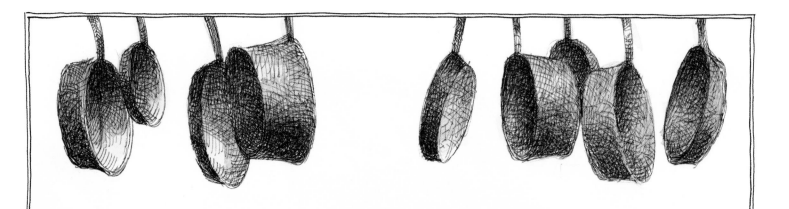

And though

it's getting

amazingly high,

there's so much

more

to American pie!

Spice
with ideas
seasoned
with dreams
and customs
from faraway lands.
Add
roaring rivers and
bubbling streams
and towns built with
strong, loving hands.

Drizzle in rays
from a glowing sunset.
Abundantly
flavor with
care.

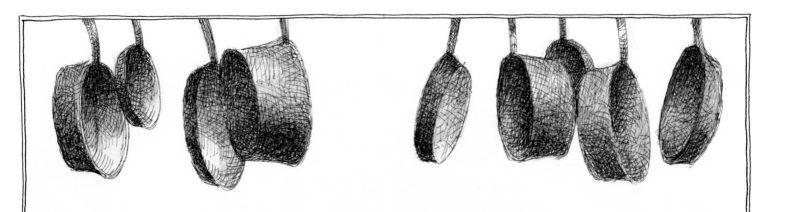

And this is **important**,
so **never forget**
to **add** some
forgiveness
to spare.

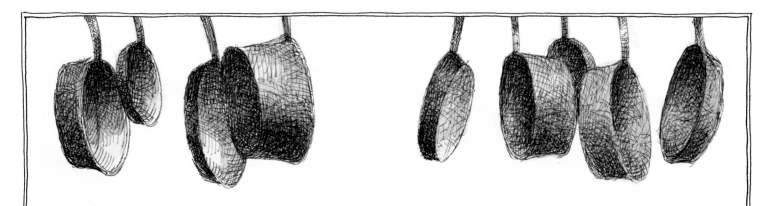

And though it's getting
**enormously
high,**
there's still even
more
to American pie!

The secret ingredients
cannot be bought,
so borrow
from Heaven above.
The key to it all
is to pour in the pot
plenty of
faith, hope, and love.

Now roll out a top
of spacious skies
to cover
this country of ours.
Place in God's grace
and allow to rise.
Then garnish
with fifty bright stars.

And that's how to **bake** an American pie
(first ever made on the **Fourth of July**).

Serves: Just as **many** who wish to stop by.